Recitations for Girls and Boys

This edition published 2025
by Living Book Press

ISBN: 978-1-76183-522-3 (hardcover)
        978-1-76183-521-6 (softcover)

A catalogue record for this book is available from the National Library of Australia

Recitations for Girls and Boys

FROM SIX TO TEN YEARS OF AGE

by

GRACE M. TUFFEY

CONTENTS

Poor Peter. 1

The Tin Soldier. 2

Looking For Treasures. 4

Red Riding Hood. 5

My Wish. 7

I Am Glad! 8

The Story of a Foolish Lamb. 9

A Short Tale About a Snail. 11

Bobby's Picnic. 13

Gathering Mushrooms. 15

The Traveller. 16

In The Park. 17

Daisies. 19

The Story of the Months. 20

The Leader. 21

Before the Storm. 22

Sunrise. 23

POOR PETER.

BILLY has gone to buy marbles,
    Purple and yellow and white,
Helen is up on the hillside,
    Flying a wonderful kite.
Michael is making an engine—
    Now he is painting it red—
But Peter is terribly grumpy,
    Because of a cold in his head...
And Mother has sent him to bed!

THE TIN SOLDIER.

IT was night-time in the nursery, and the fire was
    nearly out,
When the new tin soldier, Thomas, left the cup-
    board with a shout,
Quickly slid towards the carpet and began to march
    about.

"I'm the new tin soldier, Thomas, and my coat is
    painted red.
I've a brightly-painted helmet on my brightly-
    painted head,
I'm the pride of all the nursery. I'm a splendid toy,"
    he said.

All the cupboard doors were opened, and the dolls
    came out to stare.
"What a dreadful noise you're making!" said a wise
    old Teddy Bear.
"And why ever are you strutting up and down the
    carpet there?

"Go to bed, you foolish creature! Put your silly
    sword away!
We are tired and want to sleep now; we've been
    working all the day.
And what makes you think that you are such a
    splendid creature, pray?

"Now, suppose you were an engine, and could run
    about on wheels,
Or a nicely brought-up doll, and sat at table for
    your meals,
But a little stuck-up toy, that only struts about
    and squeals—"

Then they shut the doors up tightly, and they all
    went back to bed,
And the new tin soldier, Thomas, thought of all
    the Bear had said.
He took off his shining helmet, and hung down his
    foolish head.

Then he quietly climbed the cupboard, and he
    quietly crept inside.
"Why, I couldn't buy my breakfast with my old
    sword if I tried!
I'm a very silly soldier! I will mend my ways!" he
    cried.

LOOKING FOR TREASURES.

DAVID hunts for treasure-trove,
  Down beside the sea,
While the little dancing waves
  Splash above his knee.
Once he found a spinning-top,
  Merrily afloat,
Once he found a little tiny
  Wooden sailing boat.
David wants a rubber ball,
  Painted green and red,
But he spent his money on
  Sailors made of lead.
So he's going to look and look—
  Surely there must be
India-rubber balls afloat,
  Somewhere in the sea!

RED RIDING HOOD.

LITTLE Red Riding Hood, I understand,
Walked through the pretty wood, basket in hand.

Mother had packed inside butter and cream.
"Be quick, dear," Mother cried. "Go by the stream,

"Over the little bridge, into the wood,
Grandma is ill in bed, Red Riding Hood.

"If someone speaks to you, hurry away.
When you get home again, then you can play."

Little Red Riding Hood hurried along,
Swinging her basket and singing a song,

Till in the hedges she suddenly spied
Twelve lovely violets trying to hide.

All that her Mother had carefully said
Straightway went out of Red Riding Hood's head.

Down went the basket as fast as it could.
"Grandma will love them!" said Red Riding Hood.

While she was picking them, down on her knees,
Up came a wicked wolf out of the trees.

"Good afternoon," he said, "my little dear!
Where are you going and what have you here?"

"I'm going to see Grandma," the little girl said.
"She lives over there, and she's staying in bed."

Straightway the wily wolf ran on before,
Came up the pathway and knocked at the door.

"Come in!" cried Grandma. "I hope you're from
    town!"
In rushed the wicked wolf; gobbled her down,

Put on her nightcap, and sprang into bed.
"Wait till Red Riding Hood gets here!" he said.

In came Red Riding Hood. "Dear Grandmama,
Do you feel better? How big your eyes are!"

"The better to see you!" the old wolf replied.
"Oh, what big ears you have!" Riding Hood cried.

"The better to hear you!" the wily wolf smiled,
As he pulled up the blankets and stared at the child.

"What a big mouth!" said the child, drawing near.
"The better to gobble you up with, my dear!"

He threw off the bedclothes and sprang on the floor;
Little Red Riding Hood flew to the door;

But just as the wicked wolf jumped off the bed,
In rushed her father and chopped off his head.

MY WISH.

WHEN they're grown up, some boys I know would
    like to drive a train.
They'd drive it down to Devonshire and drive it home
    again.
They'd go at sixty miles an hour, and thunder down
    the track;
They'd drive it up to Lancashire and then they'd
    drive it back.

When they're grown up, some boys I know
    would like to sail the seas,
And right across the ocean go and land just where
    they please.
They'd have a hundred sailors bold to keep the
    decks ashine,
They'd sleep beneath the starry skies—at least,
    when it was fine!

But I don't want to sail the seas to find the
    Spanish Main,
Nor thunder down to Devonshire and thunder back
    again.
I'll tell you what I really want: my plans are all
    complete—
I want to drive a tramcar and go clanging down the
    street!

I AM GLAD!

WHEN I see the silver rain
Falling on the window pane,
    Rain in all the garden places,
    All the flowers with shining faces,
Raindrops in a silver line,
I am glad it isn't fine!

When I see the golden sun
Kiss the flowers one by one,
    Sunshine on the trees and hedges,
    Bees about the window ledges,
Sunbeams in a golden net,
I am glad it isn't wet!

THE STORY OF A FOOLISH LAMB.

A FOOLISH little lamb one day was frisking in the
    clover,
His woolley coat was white as snow, in pretty curls
    all over.

He tossed his head, and whisked his tail, and dis-
    obeyed his Mother,
And flung his heels out hard and kicked his little
    baby brother.

He said: "My coat is beautiful! My Mother's coat is
    yellow,
But mine is white as milk! Dear me! I am a splendid
    fellow!"

The Mother sheep had yellow wool, but once when
    she was younger,
And had no little lambs to watch, and keep from
    cold and hunger,

She used to skip and leap and run about the mead-
    ows early.
Her woolley coat was white as his, and quite, oh!
    quite as curly.

The foolish little lambkin thought that no one ought
    to scold him;

He only bleated scornfully at all his Mother told
    him;

But as the months went slipping past, and each
    month he grew stronger,
At last the foolish lambkin was a little lamb no
    longer.

And then one day the farmer's men came to the
    field and caught him,
And to a little running stream with other sheep they
    brought him.

Then when they'd washed his woolley coat and in
    the water dipped him,
They nearly broke his little heart because they
    closely clipped him.

He ran across the meadow, feeling very sad and
    chilly,
And bleated miserably: "Baa, Baa! Why—why was I
    so silly?

"I laughed at Mother's yellow coat, and thought I
    looked so splendid.
I little knew how very soon my triumph would be
    ended!

"I never would have been so vain and thought so
    much about it,
If I had only known how soon I'd have to go without
    it!"

A SHORT TALE ABOUT A SNAIL.

CHILD.

Where are you going to,
With your house growing, too,
    Twixt your head and your tail,
    Mr. Snail, Mr. Snail?

MR. SNAIL.

Pray do not hurry me!
Oh, how you worry me,
    Till my head's in a whirl,
    Little girl, little girl!
        or
Pray do not hurry me!
Oh, how you worry me!
    Do you think I'm a toy,
    Little boy, little boy?

CHILD.

Did I alarm you, then?
I would not harm you, then.
    Do creep in my pail,
    Mr. Snail, Mr. Snail.

Would you like it, I wonder,
If I carried you under
    The seat of my chair?
    There's a shady spot there.

MR. SNAIL.
I should quite like the ride,
    And you're certainly kind,
    But if you don't mind
I will not creep inside.

I will follow this track,
    And remain on the ground.
    It is safer, I've found,
With my house on my back!

BOBBY'S PICNIC.

WE went for a picnic on Monday,
    And Daddy was driving the horse,
(Though I shall be driving him one day,
    But Daddy will come too, of course).

The others were up in a minute,
    With plenty of room still to spare;
There wouldn't be any fun in it
    If Mother and Joan were not there.

Our lunch was packed up in a basket,
    With custard and pastries and meat.
We called it an old magic casket,
    From which we took things good to eat.

We found out a nice place to settle,
    And made up a fine fire of wood.
The fire was to boil up the kettle:
    It did it as fast as it could.

We sat nice and near to the water,
    And watched all the queer little boats.
Black Bess had the food that we brought her,
    A bag full of sweet-smelling oats.

I did wish Black Bess had a saddle,
    To take me along for a ride.
I did wish they'd say I could paddle—
    I wished heaps of wishes beside.

I longed when we drove home at night-time
    To run by the side of the wheels.
When Black Bess was tired was the right time
    To show her a clean pair of heels.

But then it began to get creepy,
    The fields were so dark and so still,
And Joan and me felt a bit sleepy,
    As we went jog-a-jog down the hill.

So we snuggled up closely to Mother,
    And watched for the stars overhead.
They peeped out one after the other
    When I was tucked safely in bed.

GATHERING MUSHROOMS.

DID you ever get up early,
　　When the sun was hardly showing,
Ever steal across the garden
　　Without anybody knowing?
Did you ever get your shoes wet,
　　As you tramped across the clover,
When you'd reached the garden fences,
　　And had vaulted safely over?

Did you ever look for mushrooms,
　　As for diamonds in a casket?
When you found them, white and gleaming,
　　Did you drop them in your basket?
Did you ever run home breathless,
　　Through the brambles, sharp and vicious?
Did your Mother, as she kissed you,
　　Cry: "My dear! These are delicious!"

THE TRAVELLER.

WHEN I leave school, I mean to go away,
And see how other people work and play.
I mean to take a ship across the sea,
(Of course, I mean the ship will carry me);
I'll go to France and Germany and Spain,
And even then I won't come home again.

I'll play at all the jolly Spanish games,
And call the Spanish children by their names.
I'll go across the mountains, and I'll see
The lovely flowers that grow in Italy.
And then I think I'll take another ship,
And go upon a little longer trip,
Where stately trees and rushing rivers are—
I'll see the lovely birds in Africa.

And last of all, because it will be best,
And even more exciting than the rest,
I'll take another ship across the seas,
And call upon the dainty Japanese.
I mean to see, as quickly as I can,
The darling little children in Japan.

IN THE PARK.

BILLY (talking to Johnny).
    I DO think it's a shame
    We cannot play a game
        Of cricket on this jolly patch of grass.

JOHNNY (to Billy).
    I say! Let's have a try,
    There's only you and I,
        And we're sure to see the old Park Keeper
pass.

LADY (who has been ill and has come
to the Park for a little air).
    Ah, here's a pleasant seat,
    I'll sit and rest my feet,
        You soon get tired of walking when you're ill.
    How nice it is to rest,
    And face the golden west,
        And see the sun go down behind the hill.
    (A ball suddenly crashes against her seat.)

LADY (jumping up in alarm).
    Good gracious! What was that?
    They have a cricket bat—
        It must have been that india-rubber ball.
    I did so want to stay,
    But if they're going to play
        It isn't safe to rest here after all.
    (She gets up wearily to go.)

PARK KEEPER (appearing suddenly and
seizing both boys by their collars).
    Now then, now then, you boys,
    That's quite sufficient noise,
        And cricket's not allowed inside the Park.
    You both deserve a thrashing
    To send that ball a-crashing—
    It's a lucky thing for you it missed the mark.
    You come along with me,
    You'll soon see where you'll be.
        It's very nice and fine to have a game
    With a tree trunk for a wicket,
    But it isn't playing cricket
        To upset a poor sick lady. *(Glaring at Johnny.)*
                WHAT'S YOUR NAME?

LADY.
    Please, Keeper, let them go.
    They're doing wrong, I know,
        But they didn't mean the ball to come my
    way.
    For when the grass is short,
    And promises good sport,
        I expect it does seem hard they cannot play.

JOHNNY AND BILLY (in chorus, as the
Keeper sets them free).
    Please, ma'am, we didn't know
    We should disturb you so,
        We saw no reason why we shouldn't play.
    We never thought of you,
    And the other people too,
        But we'll know the reason why another day!

DAISIES.

DEEP in the dewy meadow,
　　The bright-eyed daisies grow,
And butterflies of yellow
　　Among the clovers go.
The little river gurgles,
　　And splashes through the grass,
While in and out the rushes
　　The silver fishes pass.

How sweet to be a daisy,
　　To watch with open eyes
The little laughing river,
　　The yellow butterflies.
To see the fishes swimming,
　　Or timid field-mice walk
Across the dewy grasses,
　　And brush against your stalk!

THE STORY OF THE MONTHS.

In JANUARY, bleak and cold,
The year is hardly one month old.
In FEBRUARY comes the rain
To make the meadows soft again.

In MARCH the winds blow up and down,
Across the fields and through the town.
In APRIL under hedge and thorn
Pale yellow primroses are born.

In MAY the buttercups appear,
And skylarks overhead you hear.
In JUNE the sunshine lasts for hours,
The world is full of lovely flowers.

JULY brings roses red and white,
The great-winged moths fly past at night.
In AUGUST all the summer day
Through ripening corn the breezes play.

SEPTEMBER mornings quickly pass,
With mushrooms growing in the grass.
OCTOBER apples, ripe and red,
Cover the branches overhead.

NOVEMBER days grow dark and cold,
We know the year is getting old.
DECEMBER brings it to an end,
And so goodbye, Old Twelve Months' Friend!

THE LEADER.

WE live in a little white cottage,
　　Its windows look over the sea.
We've pansies and pinks in our garden,
　　Besides a red crab-apple tree.
And if you don't wear shoes and stockings,
　　To get in the way of your feet,
It doesn't take more than a minute
　　To run to the end of the street.

For that's where you come to the sandhills,
　　The sands, and the beautiful sea,
And that's where we play all the morning,
　　Boy Timothy, Mary, and me.
Boy Timothy's ever so splendid,
　　And I—well, they say I'm quite small—
So Mary is always the leader,
　　Because she's the bravest of all.

She follows and captures our steamboats—
　　The sea tries to wash them along;
She climbs to the tops of the tree-trunks;
　　She's ever so, ever so strong.
I'm wondering, when I am older,
　　And somebody else is so small,
If I shall be chosen for leader,
　　Because I'm the bravest of all.

BEFORE THE STORM.

CAN you tell me what the birds say, when they fly
    about the houses,
  When they dart among the chimney-pots, or
    underneath the eaves,
As one circles round the roof-tops, and with cries his
    mate arouses,
  When they fly together swiftly, in and out the ivy
    leaves?

Are they frightened? Are they angry? Do they talk to
    one another?
  In their funny, birdlike language are they crying
    each to each:
"It is growing dark and windy. There's a storm aris-
    ing, brother!
  We must keep beside the houses and our nests
    within our reach.

"When the happy sun has kissed her, and the world
    is bright and glowing,
  We can fly across the roof-tops underneath the
    gleaming sky,
But it's wiser when it's gloomy and a stormy wind is
    blowing
  To remain beside the houses. We are safe then,
    you and I!"

SUNRISE.

JUST before the sun has risen,
   I have paddled in the sea,
With the seagulls for my playmates,
   And the wind for company.
I have splashed across the shallows,
   When the sands stretched dark and grey,
And I've seen them turned to yellow
   At the breaking of the day.
Then the waves that crept about me
   Seemed no longer dark and cold,
For the sun had changed the waters
   To a pool of liquid gold.

I have wandered on the seashore.
   From the rushes I have heard
Frightened crying of the peewits.
   How the timid mother bird
Circles wildly round the hollows,
   Where her eggs are snugly laid,
For she thinks I've come to steal them,
   And her bird-heart is afraid.
Little frightened mother-peewit!
   If I see them on the ground,
I shall leave them as you left them,
   And you'll find them, safe and sound.